to Joshua Tejada
—S.C.

to the Kimura sisters
—S.Y.

Oopsy, Teacher!

**The artist would like to extend
a special thanks to Mikako Miyazaki**

Text copyright © 2012 by Stephanie Calmenson
Illustrations copyright © 2012 by Sachiko Yoshikawa

Carolrhoda Books
A division of Lerner Publishing Group, Inc.
241 First Avenue North
Minneapolis, MN 55401 U.S.A.

Website address: www.lernerbooks.com

Main body text set in Futura 26/33. Typeface provided by Adobe Systems.

Library of Congress Cataloging-in-Publication Data

Calmenson, Stephanie.
    Oopsy, teacher! / by Stephanie Calmenson ; illustrations by
Sachiko Yoshikawa.
        p.   cm.
    Sequel to: Late for school!
    Summary: Even Mr. Bungles the teacher sometimes has a
day when, no matter how hard he tries, everything seems
to go wrong—including allowing the class hamster,
Nibbles, to escape.
    ISBN 978–0–7613–5894–7 (lib. bdg. : alk. paper)
    [1. Stories in rhyme. 2. Teachers—Fiction. 3.
Lost and found possessions—Fiction. 4. Hamsters—
Fiction. 5. Humorous stories.] I. Yoshikawa,
Sachiko, ill. II. Title.
PZ8.3.C13Oop 2012
[E]—dc23   2011035756

Manufactured in the United States of America
1 – DP – 7/15/12

OOPSY, TEACHER!

Stephanie Calmenson

illustrations by **Sachiko Yoshikawa**

Carolrhoda Books Minneapolis

Our teacher Mr. Bungles is really very cool.

He always, always, **always** tries to do his best at ...

school!

But even the best teachers
can have an **oopsy** day.
No matter how they try,
sometimes things don't go their way.

Just the other morning,
getting out of bed,
poor Mr. Bungles
went and bumped his . . .

head.

Then he took a shower
and got soap in his eye.

Next, he ate his breakfast
and dripped jam on his . . .

tie.

At school, he took attendance and said, "Who is playing tricks? I just counted five of you. Now I'm seeing…

"six."

He went to clean out Nibbles' cage.
He opened up the door.
He had to sneeze and then—*achoo!*

Nibbles jumped down to the...

floor!

Mr. Bungles tried to catch him,
running here, running there.
Nibbles jumped from desk to desk,
then onto Mr. Bungles'...

In no time, Nibbles slipped away!
We quickly followed him—
down the stairs, across the hall.

He was heading for the...

"Hurry, children, hurry!
We must get our hamster back.

Look, he's over there!
He is jogging 'round the...

Poor Mr. Bungles
didn't see the ball.

Poor Mr. Bungles couldn't stop his...

Up again, the chase was on,
to the stairs and down.
Nibbles had the lead.
He was heading for the...

We saw him make his getaway.
We gasped as he took flight!
Our hamster sailed away
on the tail of a . . .

We lost him till we heard the yelps.
"A hamster's here!" cried Tony.
Nibbles was at his pizza place.

He was nibbling...

Mr. Bungles sat down with a sigh.
He said, "Nibbles, you're a smarty.
You ran us 'round till lunchtime.
Kids, let's have a pizza . . .

Yes, that's our Mr. Bungles.
We think he's number one!
Even with the **oopsies,**
he makes our school day...